This book belongs to

_____

_____

For Ben and Ollie

Henry Holt and Company, *Publishers since 1866*
Henry Holt® is a registered trademark of Macmillan Publishing Group, LLC
175 Fifth Avenue, New York, NY 10010 • mackids.com

Copyright © 2018 by Richard Byrne
All rights reserved.

ISBN 978-1-250-18959-2
Library of Congress Control Number 2018936447

Our books may be purchased in bulk for promotional, educational, or business use. Please
contact your local bookseller or the Macmillan Corporate and Premium Sales Department
at (800) 221-7945 ext. 5442 or by e-mail at MacmillanSpecialMarkets@macmillan.com.

First published in the United Kingdom in 2018 by Oxford University Press
First American edition, 2018
Printed in China by Leo Paper Group, Gulao Town, Heshan, Guangdong Province

10 9 8 7 6 5 4 3 2 1

THE CASE OF THE Missing Chalk Drawings

Richard BYRNE

Henry Holt and Company • New York

The chalks were having fun drawing when Mrs. Red called them in for . . .

But when the chalks came back from lunch,
they were surprised to find . . .

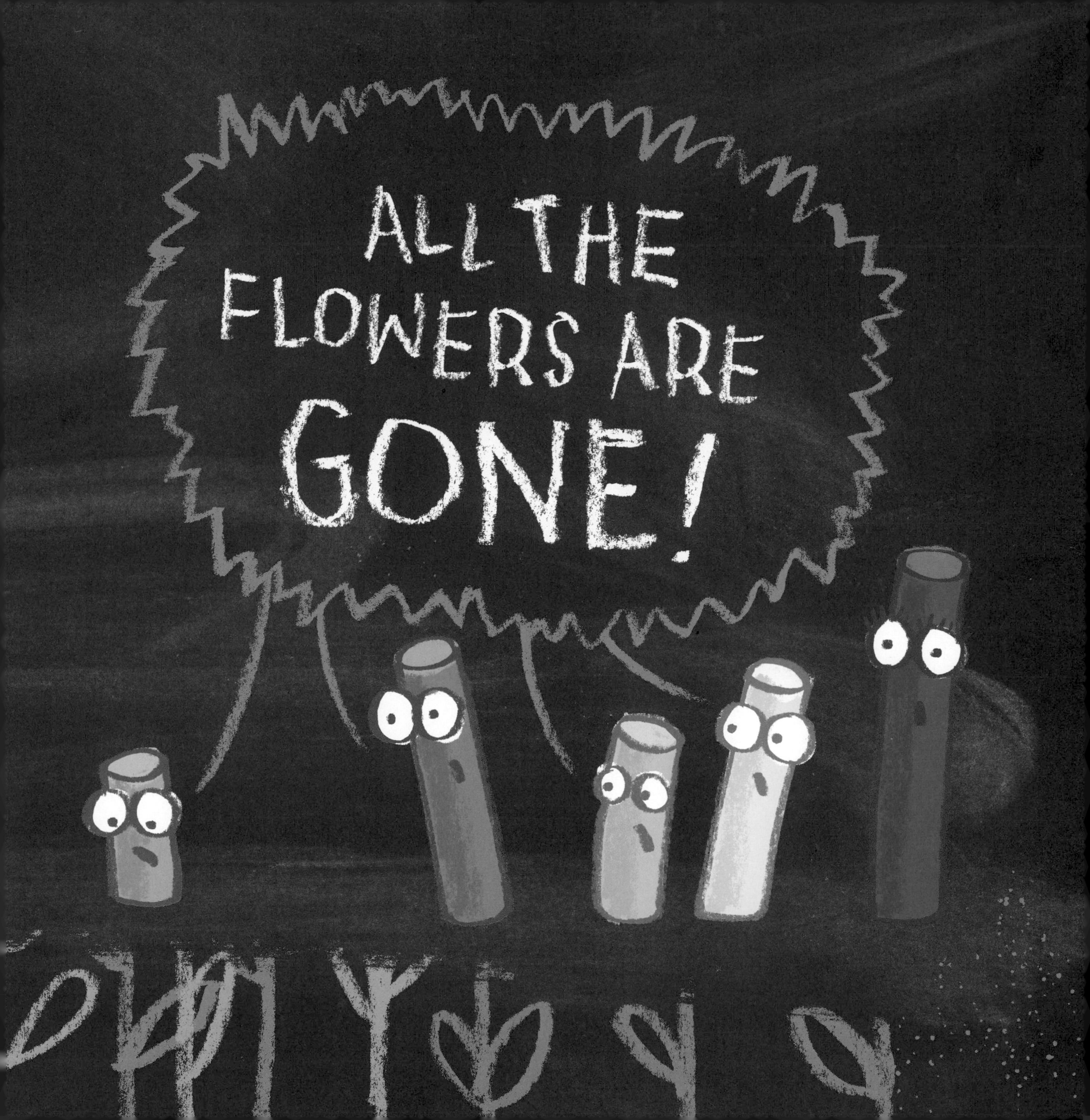
ALL THE FLOWERS ARE GONE!

The chalks started a new drawing,
but this time Mrs. Red also made a big red fence.

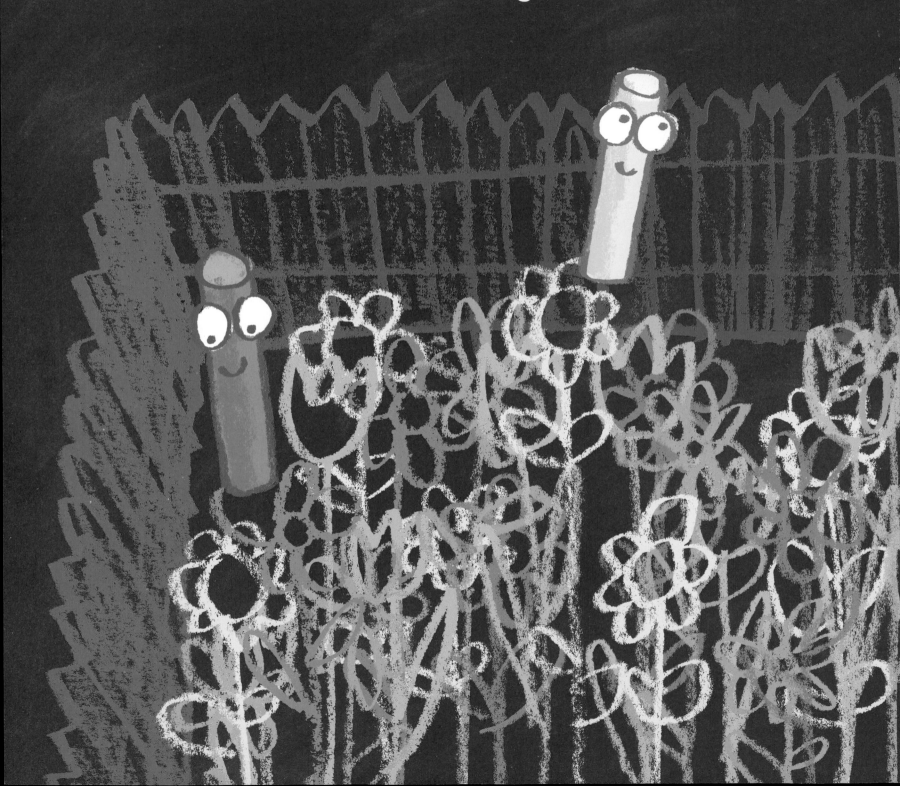

"That should keep the flowers safe while we go in for a story," she said.

But it didn't.
After story time, the flowers were gone—

and so was the fence!

SOMEONE IS STEALING OUR DRAWINGS!

Sergeant Blue arrived to investigate . . .

. . . and quickly noted some important evidence.

"The culprit is this tall

and VERY dusty!"

Sergeant Blue rounded up some suspicious-looking characters.

"Too thin.

Too small.

Too pointy.

Too
tall.

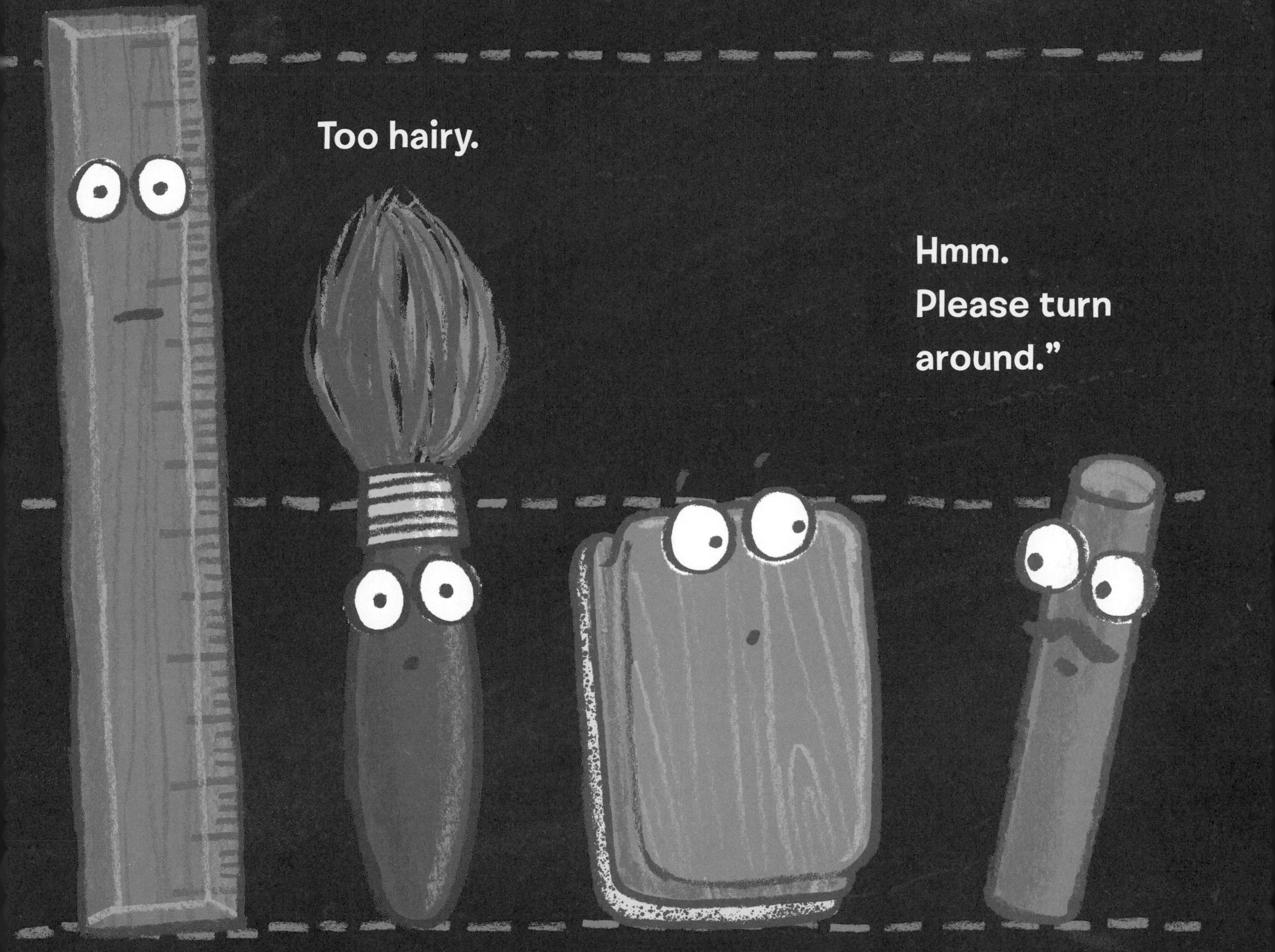

Too hairy.

Hmm.
Please turn
around."

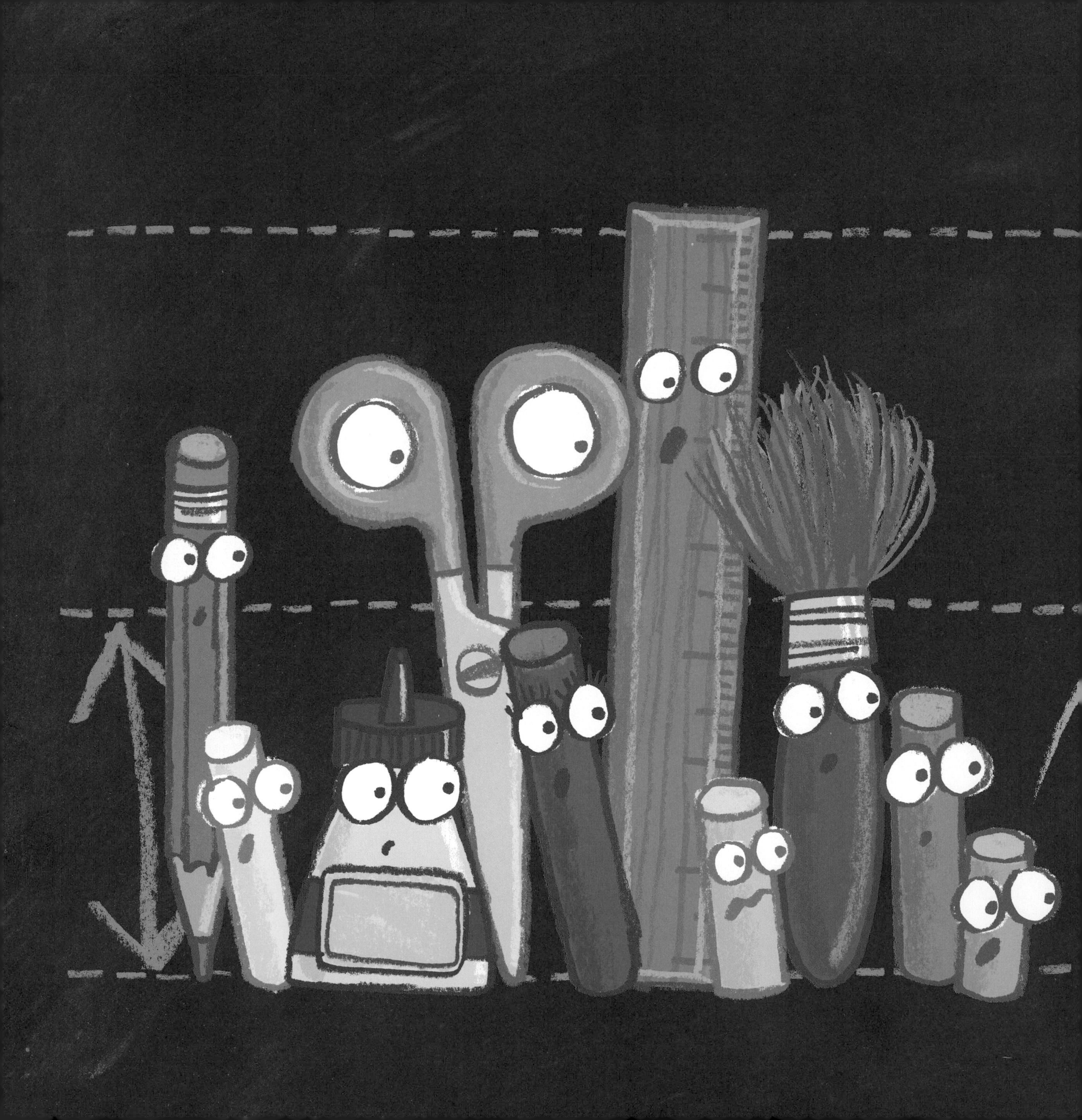

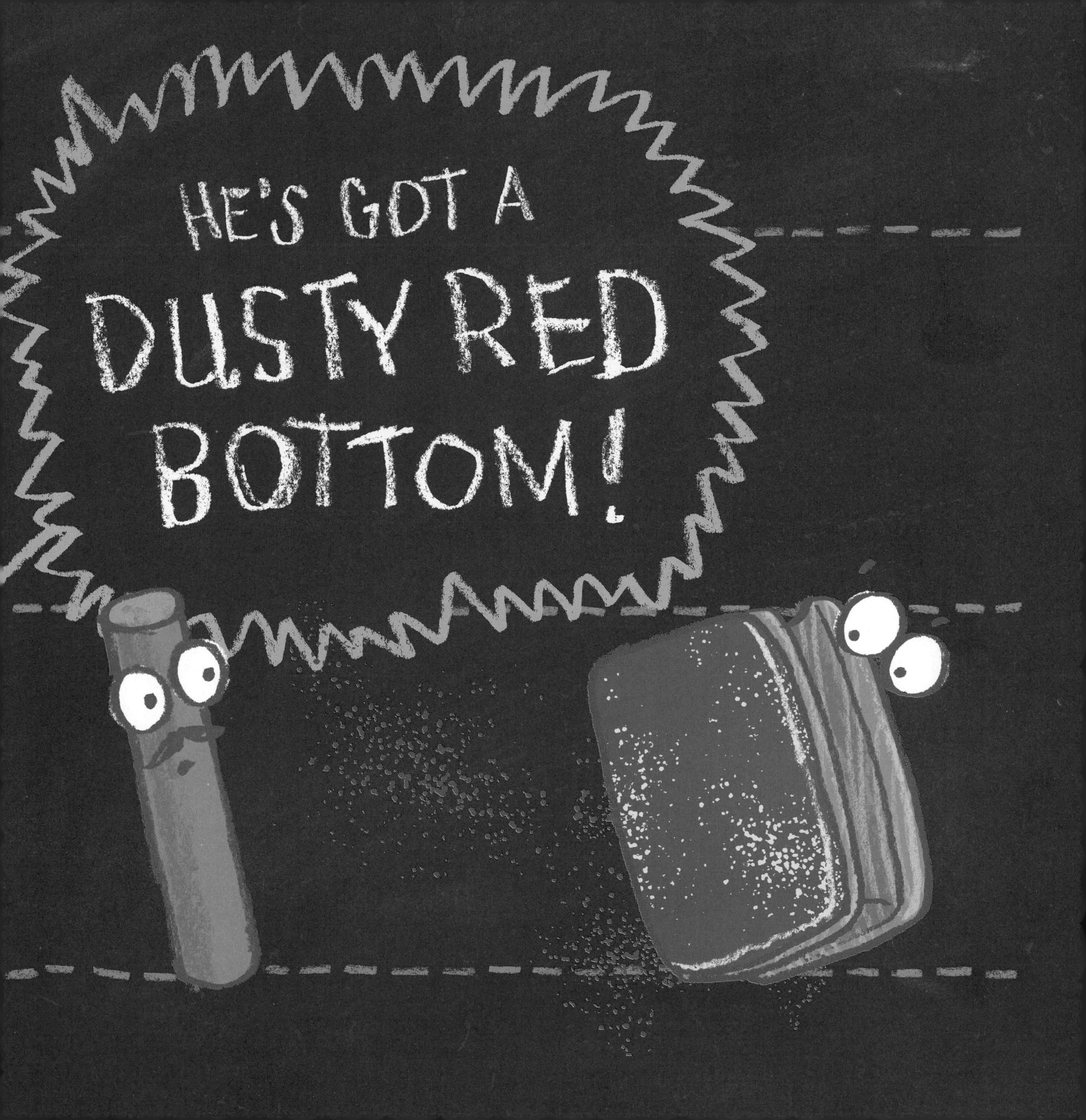
HE'S GOT A
DUSTY RED
BOTTOM!

Case closed!

But before Sergeant Blue could
put the culprit in prison . . .

. . . the robber fled in a cloud of dust.

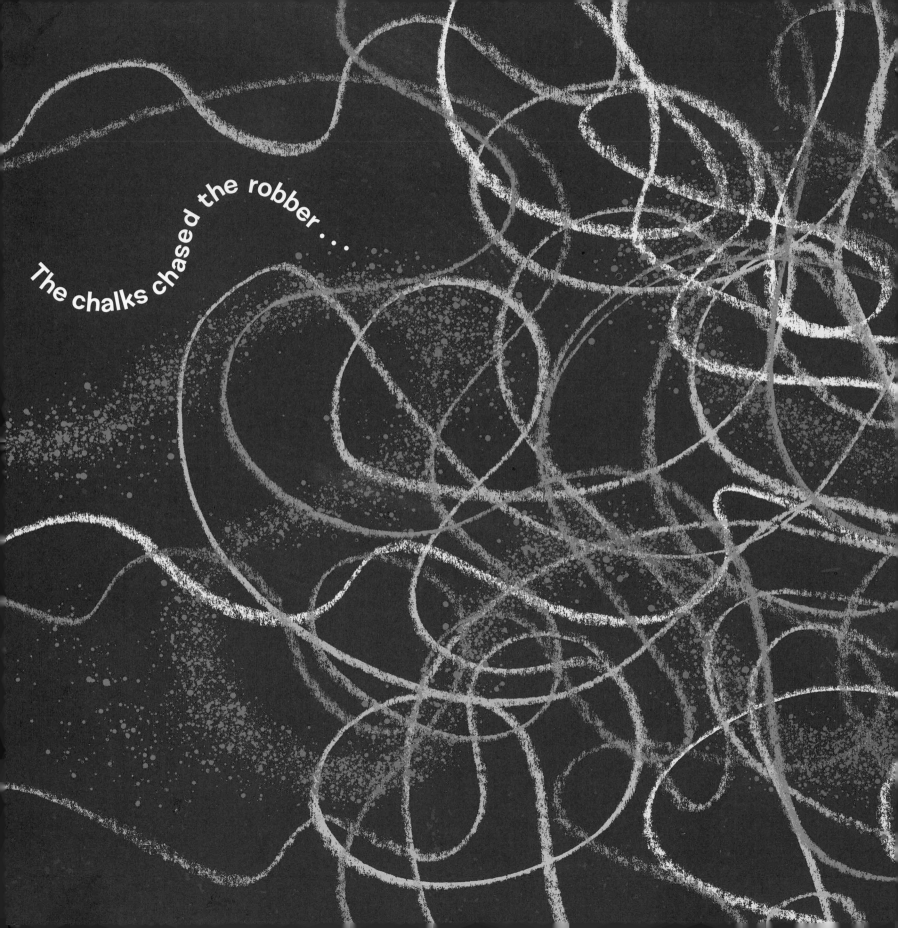

The chalks chased the robber...

. . . but they could not catch him.

The chalks were stumped.

Fortunately, Sergeant Blue
had a plan.

When the robber came upon a new drawing,
he couldn't resist.

Rainbow,
here I
come!

The chalks suddenly leaped out from their hiding places.

The chalkboard eraser felt wrongly accused.

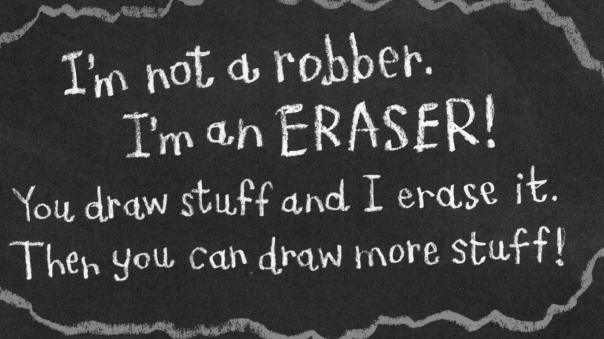

The chalks felt very guilty.
They had made
a terrible mistake.

Sergeant Blue knew how
to make things right.
They should all chase
the eraser again . . .

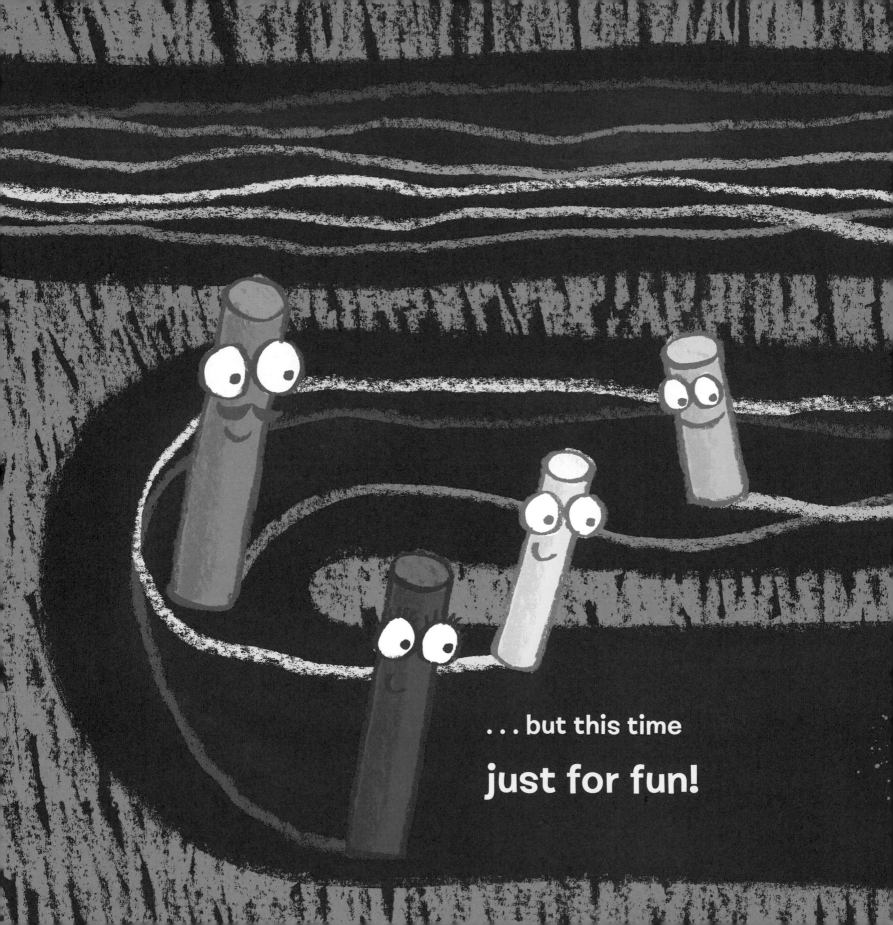

. . . but this time

just for fun!